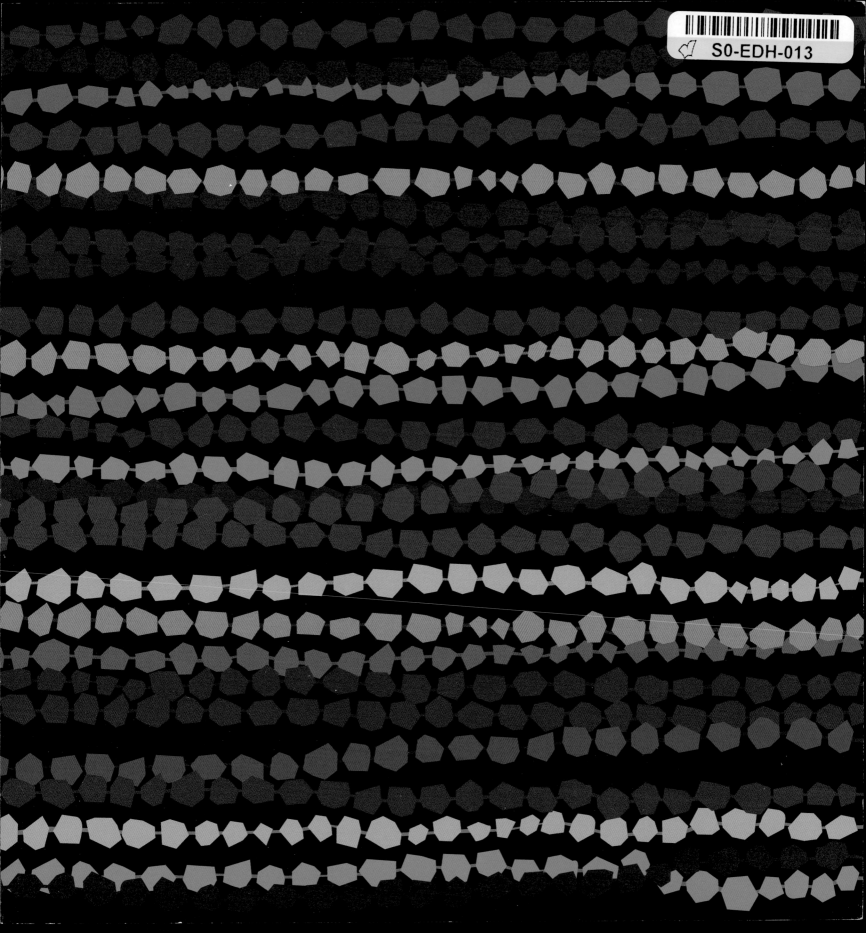

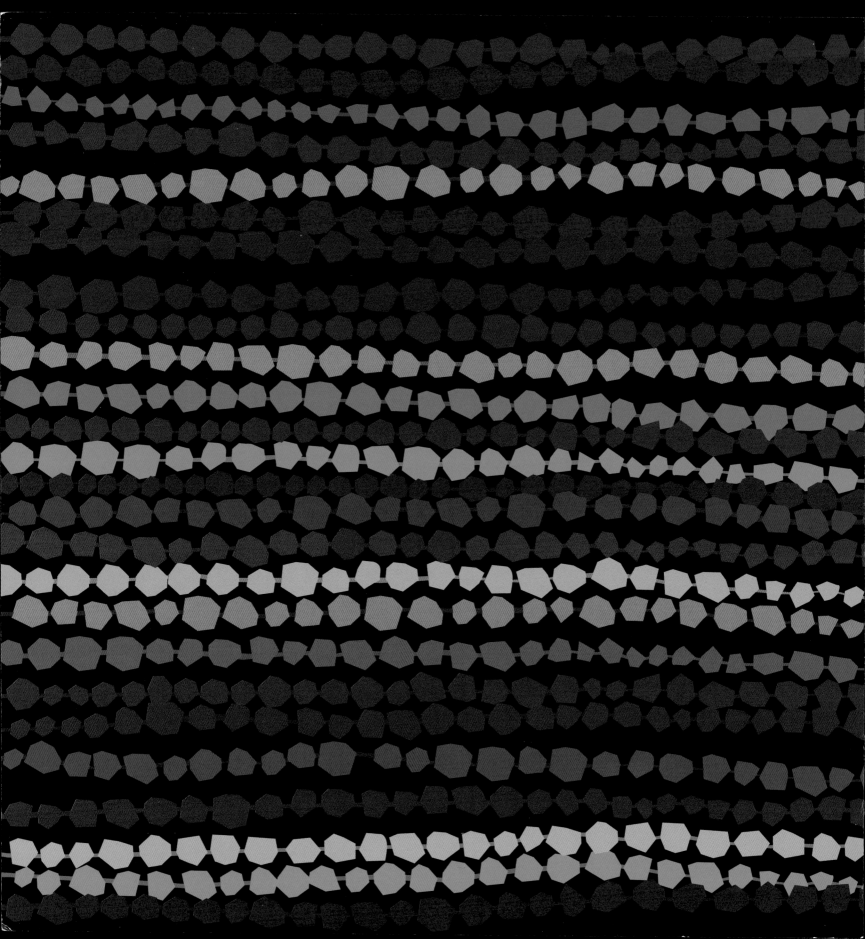

Creole Cottages

Alligator Acres

Eloise's Crib

Woo's Saw Palmettos

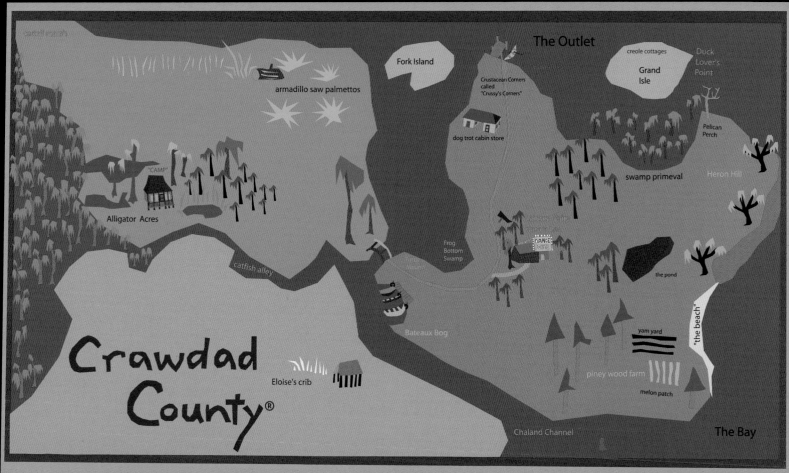

Crawdad County®

Welcome to Crawdad County, a little to the right of there and just a bit south of beyond. It's country where you'll hardly ever be out of earshot of an accordion playing, where there are always a couple of friends fishing among the sawgrass and cypress knees, and where never a night goes by when there's not a tale to tell. This is just one of those tales.

So push back your chairs, kick up your heels, and dance the night away with this spirited ballad of three winsome companions deep in bayou country.

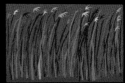

For Martha,
salsa dancer extraordinaire,
whose dancing is always inspiring.
—D. A.

In loving memory
of Honey, our grandmother,
who taught us all to dance
and in whose world
nobody was ever too big
to dance, even Mrs. Granger
and her watermelon pickles.

And for Donna Jean who
loved to play the banjo
and dance to Dudley.
—S. A.

Text copyright © 2004, 2015 Doug Anderson
Illustrations copyright © 2004, 2015 Sara Anderson
Crawdad County® is a registered trademark of Sara Anderson

All rights reserved. No part of this publication may be reproduced, stored in a
retrieval system, or transmitted in any form or by any means—electronic, mechanical,
photocopy, recording, or any other—without the prior written permission of the publisher.

This 2015 paperback edition published by
Sara Anderson Children's Books
Seattle, Washington
www.saranderson.com

Library of Congress Control Number: 2015907469
ISBN: 978-0-9702784-9-4
LP9.15-1

TOO BIG TO DANCE

Story by Doug Anderson

Illustrated by Sara Anderson

A Crawdad County® Book

Sara Anderson Children's Books
Seattle, Washington

Way back in the bayou country lies Crawdad County. The Spanish moss on the live oaks hangs so thick that unless you look especially closely, you might not notice rickety Alligator Acres, huddled cozily upon the water's edge. It's country just teeming with folks, a friendly kind of place Cecil, the alligator, calls home.

Back beyond live Cecil's neighbors, including little Woo, the armadillo, and a zebra named Eloise. Just how a zebra came to be there is a story for another time. The wind does not often blow through the steamy bayou—but when it does, a story is sure to follow. The wind is blowing tonight, there's a distant fiddle singing, and the story we are here to tell is about the Crawdad County dance—of Eloise, who didn't quite fit in, and of Cecil and Woo, who made sure that she did.

Cecil, gracious gator,
       heard the wind come singing,
Wishing it would take his cares
       and with them go a-winging.

Woo, the armadillo, settled in the grassy wind,
Hoping something nice might happen to a little guy like him.

A wind came on the bayou, distant stars began to rise.
Sweet Eloise, the zebra, got some stardust in her eyes.

Dreaming of the evening, anticipating fun,

They talk as they await the setting of the sun.

Cecil, Woo, and Eloise are stepping out tonight.
Across the beaten bayou path, southern stars are smiling bright.

A breeze was in the bayou, it was a night to take a chance,
For all who had their hearts set on the Crawdad County dance.

**Spirits were rising levee high, as the three friends came to town.
Lights were strung at the Laissez Faire, fiddles sang a Cajun sound.**

Laughs spilled deep into the night, music spread far and wide.
Cecil and Woo and some turtles, too, made their way inside.

Inside, Cecil dos-a-doed, while Woo was whisked and whirled,

Some danced stately, solemn, and straight—others tossed and twirled.

Eloise walked up to the door, her heart set on romance.

But she could not reach the hardwood floor, she was too big to dance.

While down below the dance went on, her heart was feeling blue.

Wistful Woo walked from the dance to spend a moment with her.

Cecil swung and Cecil stomped, to the drumming beat until,
He missed his little armadillo friend, and saw him standing on the hill.

Clever Cecil grabbed a squeeze box as the band behind him played.

Then out to Woo and Eloise, he led a dance parade.

So they all waltzed slow together, as the moon shone on the pond.
Large and little they did dance, as the band played "Jolie Blonde."

When the music is over in Crawdad County, when the dance is done,
There are still some stars to steal our hearts, on the other side of the sun.

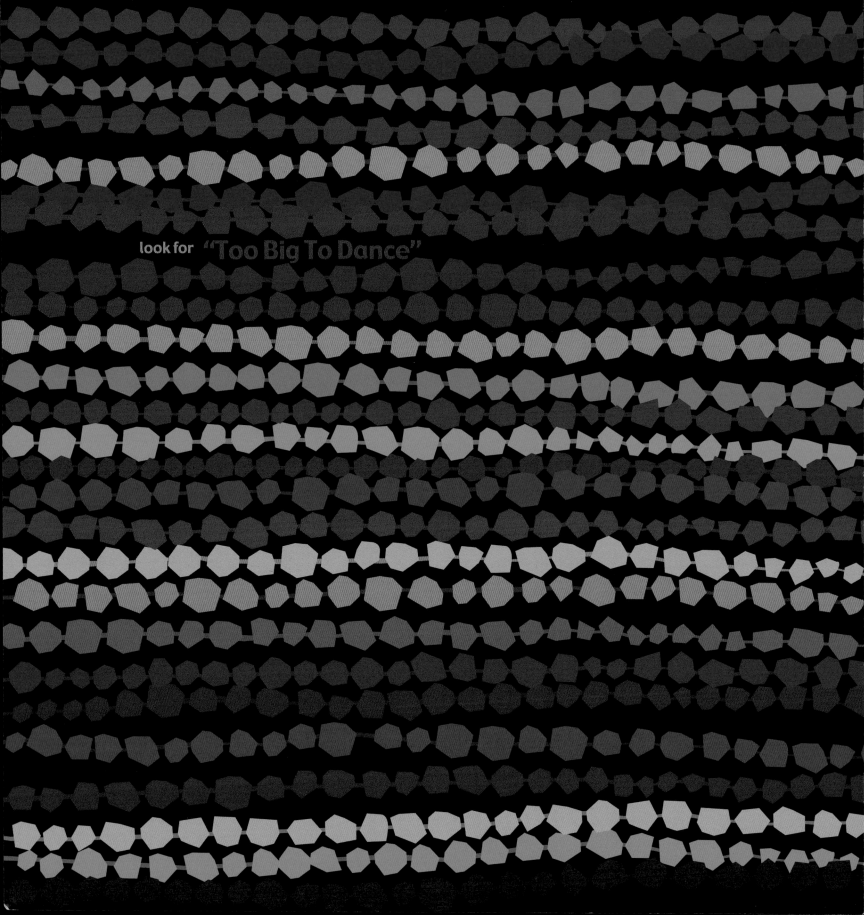

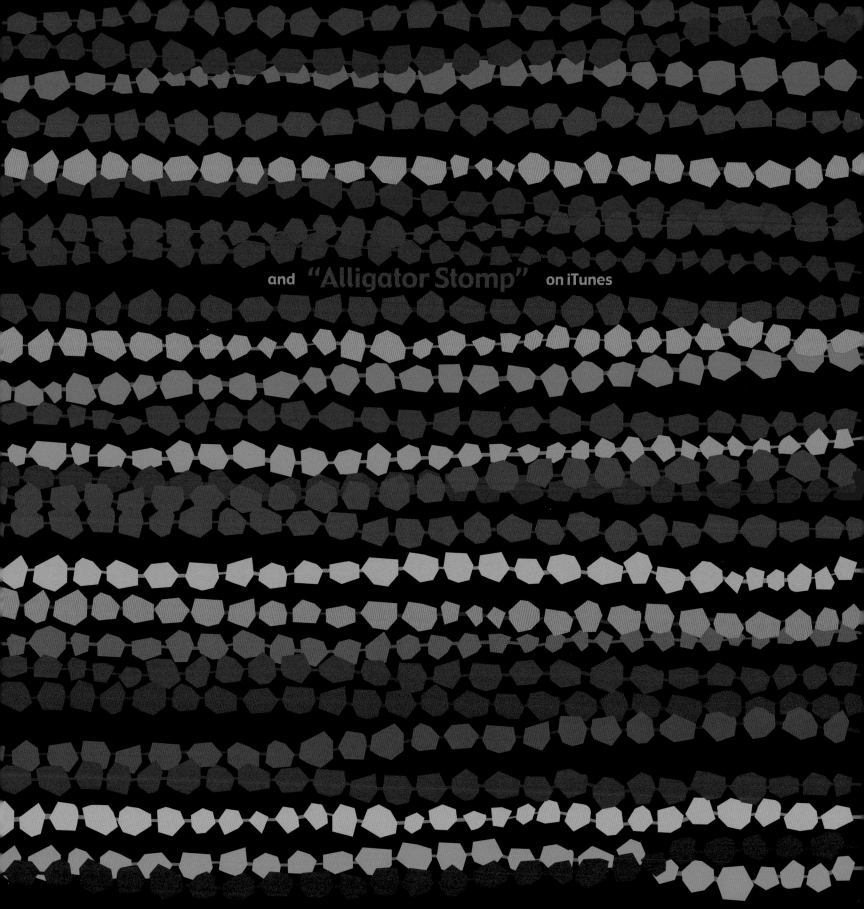

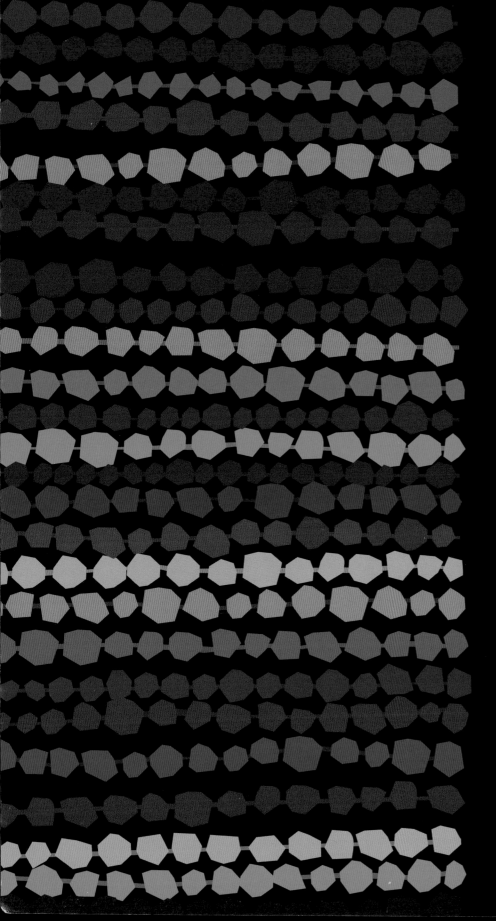

Brother and sister Doug and Sara Anderson grew up with a grandmother who had a dance band and played the banjo and the ukulele—in a family where many sang, everyone danced, and Uncle Spud played the sax.

Doug has played in various settings and genres including folk, country, rock, and jug bands. When not writing, singing, or playing (harmonica, banjo, and guitar), Doug teaches in the philosophy department at Southern Illinois University. He lives in Carbondale, Illinois with lots of dogs, cats, and guitars. For more about his music go to olmoose.com

Sara can't carry a tune in a bucket or manage dotted eighth notes, but she could always draw, and she loves to dance. Cecil, the alligator, accidentally hatched in her hands while she was working on a Christmas card for the Museum of Modern Art in New York almost thirty years ago. He grew up parallel to her career as a cut paper artist. Her other books include OCTOPUS OYSTER HERMIT CRAB SNAIL, SOME OF MY BEST FRIENDS ARE POLKA-DOT PIGS, A DAY AT THE MARKET, NOISY CITY DAY, NOISY CITY NIGHT, and the new bilingual books FRUTAS•FRUIT y VERDURAS•VEGETABLES. She lives in Seattle, Washington.

Thanks to Bruce of The Zydeco Flames for fostering a love of zydeco with tales of Lafayette and Clifton Chenier and to Queen Ida's band for many a delightful dance. Special thanks to Mama for her Christmas Gumbo and all that Louisiana love, the Mississippi Michaels for their bayou swamp grass, and Allison for a job well done. As always, a tip of the hat to our constant collaborators Martha, Marshall, and Russell.

www.saranderson.com

A Crawdad County® Book

www.crawdadcounty.com